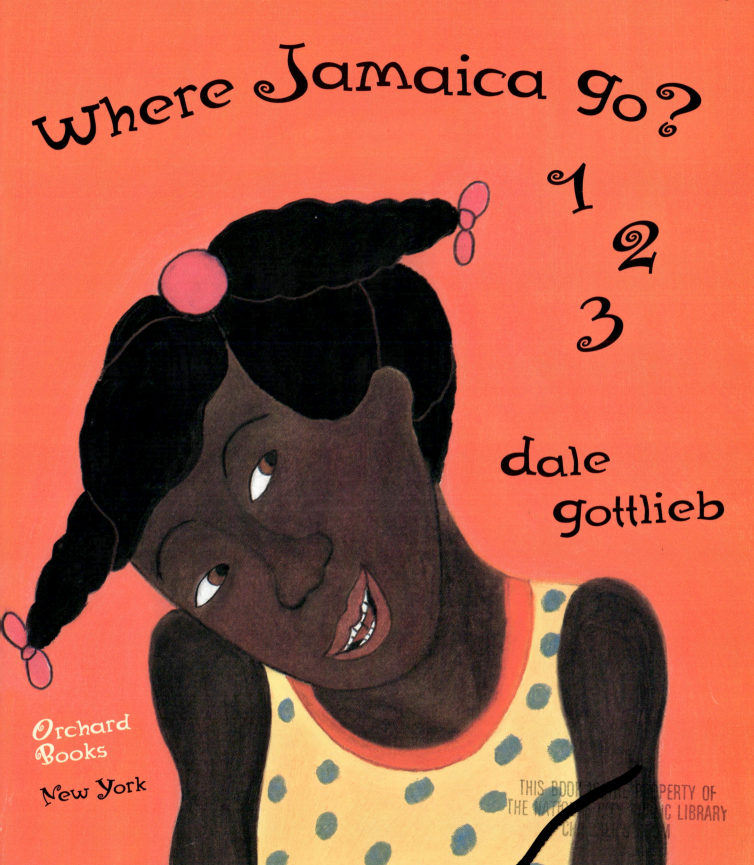

Where Jamaica go?

1
2
3

dale gottlieb

Orchard Books

New York

for
Burnsie

Text and illustrations copyright © 1996 by Dale Gottlieb

Orchard Books
95 Madison Avenue
New York, NY 10016

Manufactured in the United States of America
Printed by Barton Press, Inc.   Bound by Horowitz/Rae
Book design by Chris Hammill Paul

10   9   8   7   6   5   4   3   2   1

The text of this book is set in 36 point Mex Regular.   The illustrations are oil pastel.

Library of Congress Cataloging-in-Publication Data

Gottlieb, Dale, date.
        Where Jamaica go? / Dale Gottlieb.
            p.   cm.
        "A Melanie Kroupa book"—Half t.p.
        Summary: Jamaica has fun and sees many colorful sights as she goes downtown,
goes beachcombing, and rides home with Daddy.
        ISBN 0-531-09525-8. — ISBN 0-531-08875-8 (lib. bdg.)
        [1. Caribbean Area—Fiction.] I. Title.
    PZ7.G696Wh   1996
    [E]—dc20   96-3997

Jamaica 1

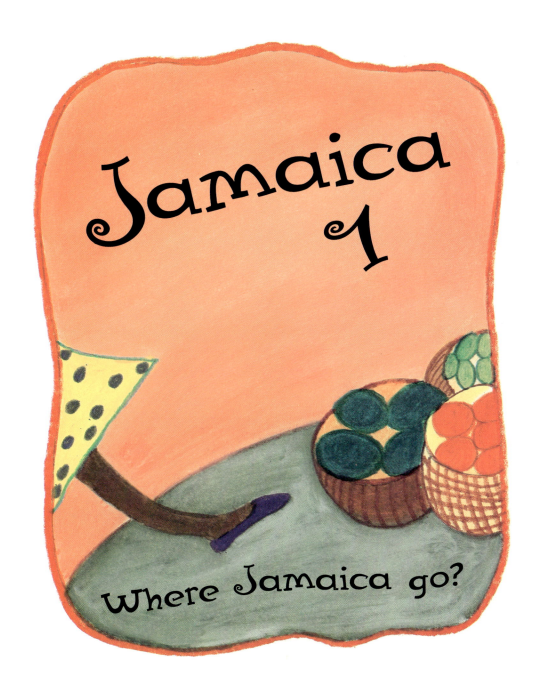

Where Jamaica go?

Fish and fruits and

Miss Lee Brown.

What
Miss Lee Brown
do?

She do the drums. She play them funny?

Go tum tee tum!

What Jamaica do
when she see Miss Brown?

Clap and tap and dance around.

Everybody watch
in this ol' town.

Jamaica make 'em laugh and lose their frowns.

Jamaica
2

Where Jamaica go?

Where Jamaica go?

She go beachcomb.

She take her shovel.
She bring it from home.

What Jamaica see
when she go beachcomb?

Shells and Manny and blue sea foam.

What
sea foam
do?

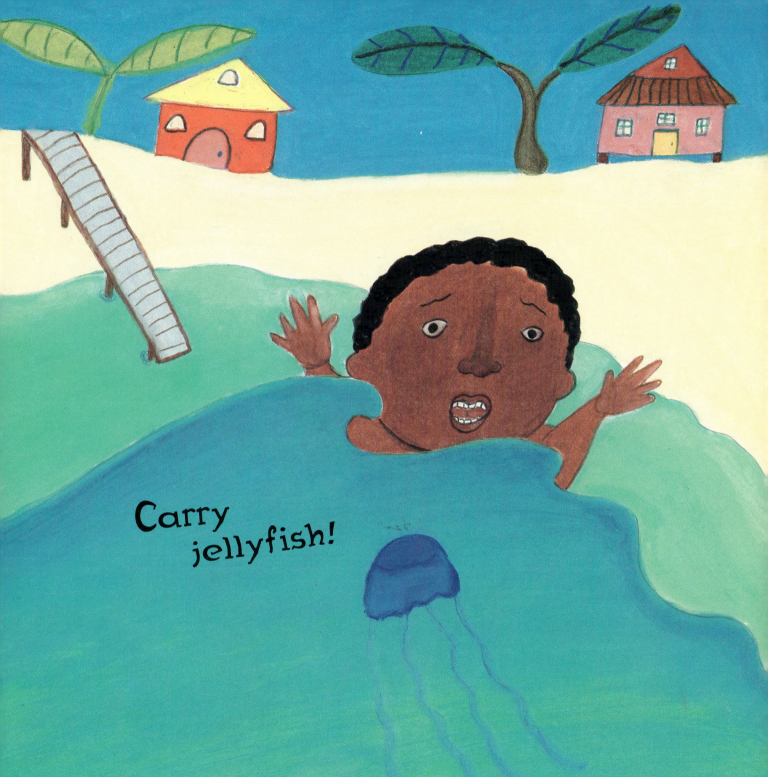

Carry
jellyfish!

What Manny do
when he see these fish?

He scared and run.
Go swish, swish, swish.

Jamaica come and look.
Big jellyfish!

Jamaica
make him
laugh.

She blow it a kiss.

Jamaica
3

Where Jamaica go?

Where Jamaica go?

She go back home.

She get there walking?

Her daddy's
Chrome Dome.

What Jamaica bring on
the ride back home?

Chickens,
books,
and
jasmine
cologne.

What Jamaica do
with this sweet
smellin' stuff?

Chase the chickie
down the road
and say,

"Come now, Miss!"

Chickie flap
and
flutter,

chickie run away.

She's not stopping for Jamaica.

She got other plans today!

Jamaica chase the chickie
all the way home.

Daddy laugh and laugh
in his big Chrome Dome.